BABYMOUSE
BEACH BABE

BY JENNIFER L. HOLM & MATTHEW HOLM

HarperCollins *Children's Books*

SKIP THIS PAGE. TRUST ME.

First published in the U.S.A. by Random House Children's Books in 2006
First published in paperback in Great Britain by HarperCollins Children's Books in 2006

10 9 8 7 6 5 4 3 2 1
ISBN-13: 978-0-00-722449-4
ISBN-10: 0-00-722449-4

HarperCollins Children's Books is a division of HarperCollins Publishers Ltd.

Visit our website at: www.harpercollinschildrensbooks.co.uk

Printed and bound in China

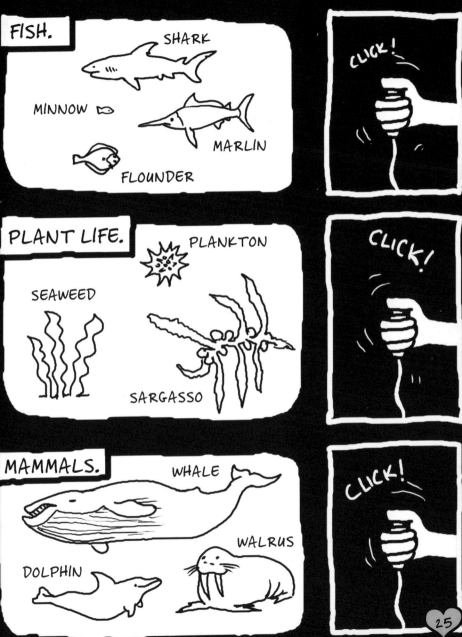

THAT NIGHT AT DINNER.

GUESS WHERE WE'RE GOING FOR OUR HOLIDAY, BABYMOUSE?

HOLIDAY?

BABYMOUSE REMEMBERED LAST SUMMER'S "HOLIDAY".

THE ACCOMMODATION.

I HEAR A BEAR!

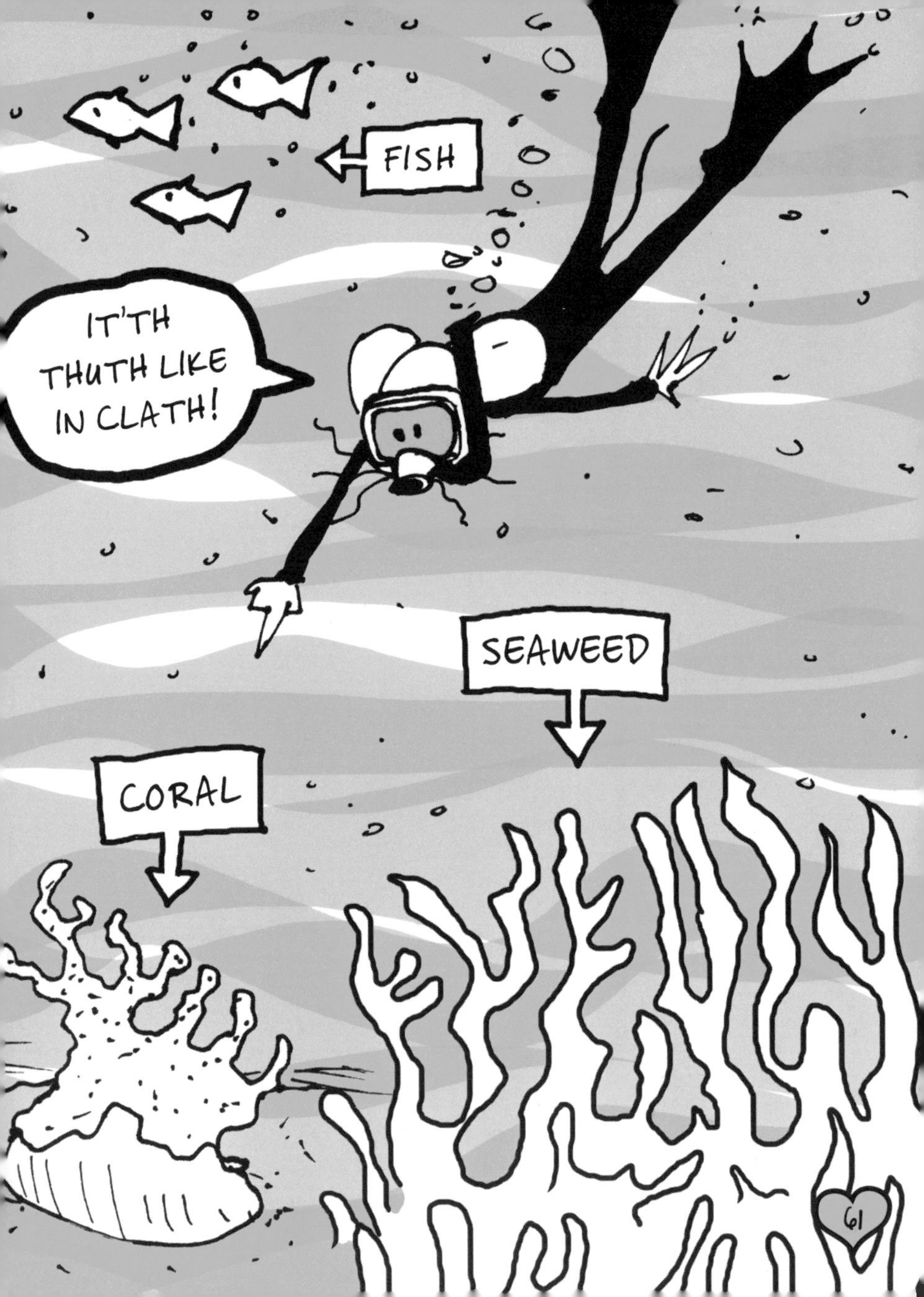
FISH
IT'TH THUTH LIKE IN CLATH!
SEAWEED
CORAL

SO WHAT'S ON THE AGENDA TODAY, BABYMOUSE?

I'M GOING TO COLLECT SHELLS!

AND NO, SQUEAK, YOU CAN'T COME.

THAT'S A PRETTY ONE!

HEY!

SNAP!

73